"I was born in London in 1946 and grew up in a sweet shop in Essex. For several years I worked as a graphic designer, but in 1980 I decided to concentrate on writing and illustrating books for children.

My wife, Annette, and I have two grown-up children, Ben and Amanda, and we have put down roots in Suffolk.

I haven't recently counted how many books there are with my name on the cover but Percy the Park Keeper accounts for a good many of them. I'm reliably informed that they have sold more than three million copies. Hooray!

I didn't realise this when I invented Percy, but I can now see that he's very like my mum's dad, my grandpa. I even have a picture of him giving a ride to my brother and me in his old home-made wooden wheelbarrow!"

NICK BUTTERWORTH

ON THE COVER

Percy says: "An ice-cream cone is just what you need on a hot, sunny day . . . especially if you're wearing a black fur coat and you can't take it off!"

PERCY'S FRIEND
THE MOLE

NICK BUTTERWORTH

Collins

An imprint of HarperCollinsPublishers

THE MOLE REALLY LIKES...

Swimming! He's surprisingly good at it too.

Spaghetti. As a special treat, I made some
for his birthday. I'm not sure if he thinks it's
food or a game, because he said, "Can we
play spaghetti at my next birthday?"

PERCY'S FRIEND
THE MOLE

NICK BUTTERWORTH

Collins

An imprint of HarperCollinsPublishers

Thanks Graham Daldry. You're a wizard.

Thanks Atholl McDonald. You're a hero!

First published in Great Britain by HarperCollins Publishers Ltd in 2002

1 3 5 7 9 10 8 6 4 2

ISBN: 0 00 711981 X

Text and illustrations copyright © Nick Butterworth 2002
The author asserts the moral right to be identified as the author of the work.

The HarperCollins website address is: www.**fire**and**water**.com

Printed and bound in Belgium

MY FRIEND
THE MOLE

The mole spends a lot of his
time under the ground but
then, all of a sudden, he'll pop up when
you least expect him. He usually wears one
of two faces. One is smiley. The other looks
confused.

We get on well, although we had to have
words when he made molehills all over my
grass. Now he understands that there are
certain places where I don't want him to dig.
And I understand that sometimes he loses his
way and digs there anyway.

The mole says he has a
secret friend called Tootie.
He says that Tootie is
very clever, but as I have
never actually met Tootie,
I couldn't say.

The mole doesn't see as well as the other animals. It doesn't really matter because he spends so much time where it's dark.

He has this funny idea that dark glasses are for helping to see in the dark. He found these plastic sunglasses somewhere in the park. I think he wears them sometimes when he's digging tunnels.

The fox told him he would be cool in them. But when the mole wore them in the sunshine he said they didn't work. He didn't feel cool. He felt hot.

THE MOLE REALLY LIKES . . .

Swimming! He's surprisingly good at it too.

Spaghetti. As a special treat, I made some
for his birthday. I'm not sure if he thinks it's
food or a game, because he said, "Can we
play spaghetti at my next birthday?"

THE MOLE DOESN'T LIKE . . .

Snow. He doesn't mind the cold, but he says it's actually harder to dig through snow than tunnelling underground. I didn't realise that.

Pepper. He has a sensitive nose, poor chap!

The mole is a very kind little chap. When he heard that I had broken my pencil, he decided to get one for me that wouldn't break.

He made it out of an old broom handle.
It doesn't actually write, because the point
is only painted on. But it looks very nice
and it's very, very long. And it certainly
won't break!

I've got lots of pictures in my photo album.

The mole is very good at doing head-over-heels. He can even do it in his tunnels. (Perhaps that's why he so often loses his way!)

The fox thought he had a black snowball - but it was furry - and it had a pink nose!

Here are some I took of my good friend, the mole.

A hot day and a special drink for a special friend.

I was told that Tootie made these muddy footprints. She might be clever, but she doesn't wipe her feet properly.

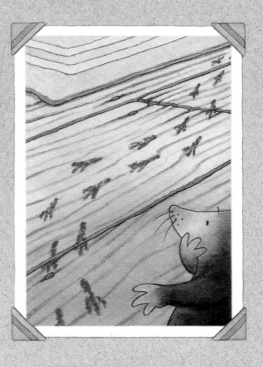

The Mole isn't afraid of the
dark, but one evening
I heard him talking to
someone who was.

"Yes, Tootie," he said, "it
does look like a monster now.
But what was it before it got dark?"

A little voice, that sounded just a bit like
the mole's, said, "A tree."

Then the mole said, "Well, that's what it
still is. A tree."

Very sensible, I thought.

When I went to say hello
to them, Tootie had gone.

THREE

The mole could never
Possibly,
Count up to more than
One, two, three.
That's why his molehills
Are so many.
He loses count at
Hardly any.
Though forty-nine
There may well be,
The mole will tell you,
"There are three!"

FAVOURITE PLACES

Most of the mole's favourite places are underground and rather dark. He says he likes them because they're cosy and small.

I think I know what he means. On a cold winter's night I like to curl up in my bed with the covers pulled tightly round me.

Actually, I can remember one very cold snowy night when the mole ended up snuggled up in my bed with me. You may have heard about it!

One place I know the mole does like is the badger's home in the big tree house. They enjoy talking together about...you guessed it...digging!

The mole doesn't live in the tree house. He has several homes nearby. But now and then he can be tempted to visit some of the other animals who live higher up in the tree.
(If you turn over the page you will
see what I mean!)

Here he is, my friend the mole.
I think this squirrel is taking him
to see the view from the top of the
tree. The mole looks like he would
rather have his feet on the ground!

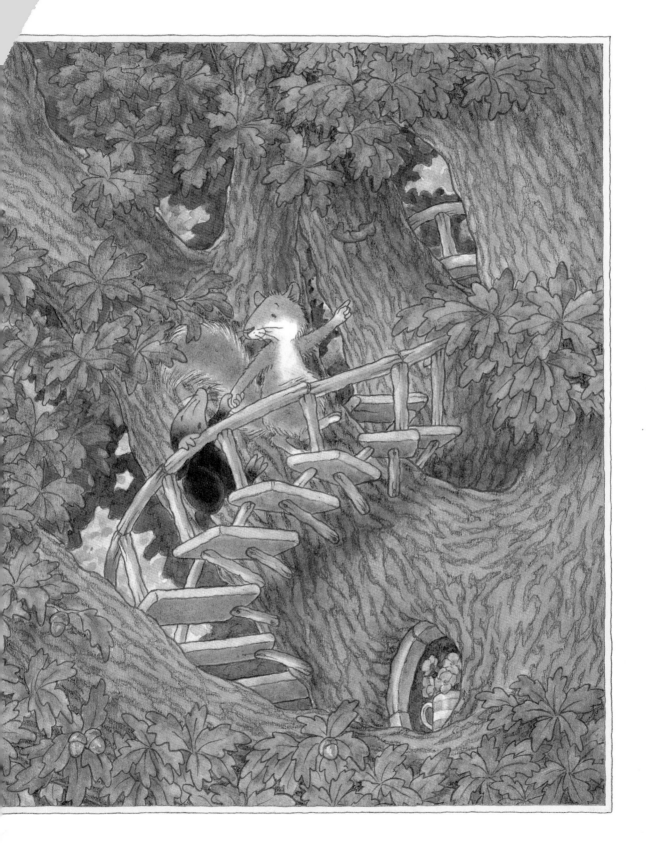

THE TREE HOUSE

In this picture you'll see Percy the Park Keeper and his friends. But if you look very carefully, you can also find a balloon, a kite, a hot-water bottle, a model aeroplane, a paintbrush, a robin, a beach ball, a magpie, a yo-yo, Percy's stripy mug, a pencil, a conker, Percy's watering can, a cheese roll, a framed picture of Percy, one of Percy's gardening gloves, a model yacht, a plastic duck, a banana, and a frog. Oh, and ten ladybirds!

FREE GIANT POSTER

Nick Butterworth's new, giant picture of the tree house
in Percy's Park shows Percy and all his animal friends
in and around their tree house home. There are also
lots of things hidden in the picture. Some are easy
to find. Some are much harder!

To send off for your free poster, simply snip off
FOUR tokens, each from a different book in the
Percy the Park Keeper and his Friends series and send them
to the address below. Remember to include
your name, address and age.

Percy Poster, Children's Marketing Department,
HarperCollins Publishers, 77-85 Fulham Palace Road, London W6 8JB

Offer applies to UK and Eire only. Available while stocks last.
Allow 28 days for delivery.

Read all the stories about Percy and his animal friends...

Percy toys and videos
are also available.